To: James
A magical story
for a magical you

From: Auntie Steph
+ UNCLE J.P. xoxo

Oh no!
The wizards
were in
BIG trouble!

A wicked witch had cast
an evil spell completely covering
their magical kingdom in
slimy and extremely smelly goo!
ALL of the wizards were trapped!

4

The wizards really needed someone to help them catch the wicked witch, but **who?**

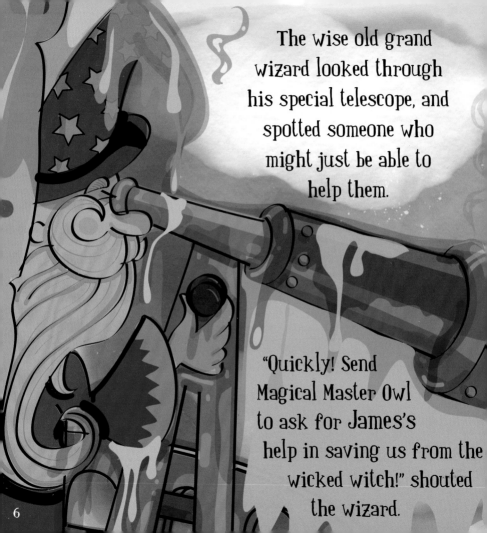

The wise old grand wizard looked through his special telescope, and spotted someone who might just be able to help them.

"Quickly! Send Magical Master Owl to ask for James's help in saving us from the wicked witch!" shouted the wizard.

Magical Master Owl knew he had
to help so he flapped and fluttered
as swiftly as he could to find the boy
spotted through the telescope.

7

"WHIZZ BAM !"
James said, as he waved his pretend wand towards his dog Ruffles.

"Oh Ruffles you are supposed to turn into a **flying dog.**"

James **SO** wanted to be a Wizard.

Suddenly
with a flitter and
a flap, Magical
Master Owl
squawked through James's
window into the bedroom and
explained (in his best owlish) the
trouble the wizards were in, and
asked a shocked James
if he could help.

9

"Of course!"
said a delighted James.

So Magical Master Owl squawked
three times, flapped his wings
four times, and with a WHIZZ
PUFF, a broomstick, cape and
magic wand suddenly appeared!

10

James put on the cape,
picked up the wand,
and jumped on his brand
new broomstick.

Quick as a flash
they zoomed out of
James's window to look
for the wicked witch.

11

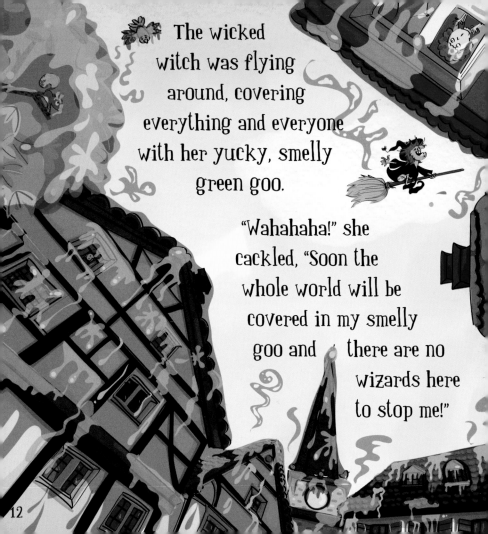

The wicked witch was flying around, covering everything and everyone with her yucky, smelly green goo.

"Wahahaha!" she cackled, "Soon the whole world will be covered in my smelly goo and there are no wizards here to stop me!"

12

But little did she realise that James was on his way.

He zoomed under bridges...

...and over houses, looking for the goo-spreading witch.

Suddenly Ruffles made
a big booming **bark**.
His super-smelling nose had caught
a whiff of the wicked witch, but she
was too far away for James
to cast a spell on her.

James clicked his heels, gripped his broomstick even tighter, and zoomed at supersonic speed towards the wicked witch.

Finally James caught up with the wicked witch.

"Who are you?" the wicked witch sneered, as she launched a **massive** dollop of **sticky** green goo at James.

With lightning speed
James waved his magic wand.
"BIZZ POP GOO I will stop you!" he shouted.
A huge brightly-coloured umbrella appeared,
deflecting all of the smelly goo.

17

The wicked witch squealed with anger, zapping another dollop of smelly green goo towards James.

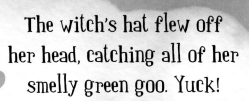

"WHIZZ SPLAT send me your hat!" James shouted.

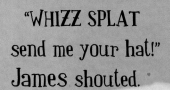

The witch's hat flew off her head, catching all of her smelly green goo. Yuck!

The witch couldn't believe what this boy wizard was doing!

"ZIP ZAP, you will be trapped in your hat!" James cast another spell.

The witch's goo-filled hat flew back to her, squashing down over her head, squishing her in the smelly green goo.

Hurray the WICKED WITCH was trapped!

A triumphant James took the wicked witch back to the wizards' castle.

All the slippery, slimy green goo had now gone thanks to James breaking the bad witch's horrible spell.

The wizards were so grateful to
James that they let him keep the cape,
broomstick AND magic wand!

James finally felt like a true wizard!

The End

COLOUR ME IN

____'S
BOOK OF
SPELLS